MY SUGAR

WHEELS & HOGS GARAGE
BOOK 5

D.M. EARL

Copyright @ 2020 D. M. Earl
Published by D. M. Earl

All rights reserved. Except for use in any review, the reproduction or utilization of this work in whole or in any part in any form by any electronic, mechanical or any other means, now or hereafter invented including photocopying, recording, information storage and retrieval systems-except in the case of brief quotations embodied in the critical article or reviews-without permission in writing from the author. This book may not be resold or redistributed without the express consent of the author.

For any questions or comments please email the author directly at DM@DMEARL.COM

This book is a work of fiction. All characters, events and places portrayed in this book are products of the author's imagination and are either fictitious or are used fictitiously. Any similarity to real persons, living or deceased is purely coincidental and not intentional.

This book contains sexual encounters, consensual and graphic language that some readers may find objectionable. It contains graphic material that is not suitable for anyone under the age of 18.

Romantic Erotic Mature Audience.

CHAPTER ONE

DES

Watching Trinity scroll through the different websites is making my head spin. Standing directly behind her while she does her search, both Cadence and Wolf sit across from us acting like the assholes they are.

"Des, how about one of those Sybaris joints? There should be enough visual stimulation to get your shit up and working at your age."

Cadence cracks himself up and starts giggling like a bitch. Wolf is trying hard not to burst into laughter; even Trinity fights not to laugh. She does let out the snort she can't hold in, which turns into her shoulders shaking with her giggles.

"I'm glad y'all find it funny I want to take care of my woman. Cadence, when you went for that couple's pedicure a couple of weeks ago with Trinity, did I give you shit? No, I commended you on being a supportive husband."

At my words Wolf lets loose, bellowing with uncontrollable laughter.

"Dude, you went to a girly place and had your 'toes' done? Goddamn, that is worse than letting lil' Hope paint them hot pink in the summer. Damn, the guys lost it then can't fuckin' wait until the guys hear this, they are gonna lose their shit."

Wolf grins Cadence's way as the kid shifts in his seat uncomfortably.

"Fuck, Des, you said that would stay between us. Son of a bitch, the guys will never let me live this shit down. Fuck and I was even thinking of going again, 'cause Trinity said if I go with her again I would get a reward. Just thinking my feet have never been so smooth and soft and can't even begin to tell you how the pedicure chair felt, made my back feel like a million bucks."

As we all start laughing hysterically, Cadence finally realizes what he had divulged and turns a shade of red I've never seen before on someone's face. That makes us all laugh even harder, including Trinity. And for her to laugh so hard being pregnant, I just know this is coming when she pushes up from my desk, trying to run-waddle, screaming like a banshee. God save us all, for Christ's sake.

"Damn it, Cadence, I got to pee. You better pray to God Almighty I make it to the restroom this time. I don't have any extra clothes to change into again. Your babies are pressing on my bladder constantly. This isn't fair at all. No more babies after these two and this time I mean it."

As she pushes out the door of my office, all three of us continue to hold our guts and howl like crazy men. And, damn, it feels fucking awesome. So much of our daily lives is pressing down on all of us and sometimes a good chuckle doesn't only brighten your day but also releases some of the stress bearing down on ya. That is my hope for taking Dee Dee away for the weekend. Get away from the hustle and bustle. Relax and just enjoy ourselves. And maybe even get me some. Yeah, I'm a dude with one thing on my mind. Fuckin' sex. Well, most of the time only one thing, sometimes I mix it up but it still ends with, yep, sex.

Wolf pushes up from his seat and takes Trinity's spot in front of the computer. As he starts pushing keys, I'm still amazed the big dude is so fluent in computers. I'm lucky to be able to find Google after typing with my two index fingers. I watch as his fingers fly over the keyboard like crazy. So involved in watching his hands I don't see the screen until he points, telling me to look at it.

"Des, check this place out. It's for couples but is a bit different. More serene and private. There are different types of cabins and you pick the one that fits your '*style.*' Some much more romantic than others. Wow, look at this one, it is fuckin' fancy. They have all kinds of outdoor activities too, like fishing, horseback riding, communal firepits, and hiking just to name a few things. And it is close enough to town that you and Dee Dee can hit the town and go shopping or get a really nice dinner. That is if you even have any intentions to leave your cabin."

As I browse through the website, I realize this is exactly what I'm looking for. Not too far from home but far enough to take my woman's mind off all the shit that is our lives. With work, the kids, and the bullshit of day-to-day, she needs a break from it all. Especially Daisy. Those two have been going at it since, shit, I don't know, it seems like forever. Especially over the holidays as it started at Thanksgiving, if I remember correctly. As her man, it's my job and I need to step in and give her some solace. And that is what I'm gonna do. I continue to look until I find the cabin that is farthest away from the lodge and after reviewing it, reach for my wallet. This is the one hands down. I throw my credit card on the desk within reach for Wolf.

"Wolf, book this for me for next weekend. This

cabin and, if possible, add some champagne and snacks for when we arrive. Oh, and some flowers too. Make sure it has some roses and orchids as those are Dee Dee's favorites."

Both men stare, their mouths hanging open in my direction. Okay, I'll give into their shock goddamn it. I know deep down in my gut I'm a decent guy but most think of me like a *'real man,'* not one who shows he can be very romantic if the mood hits me. Dee Dee knows this of course, but it's not something I advertise. Why would I, got a reputation to keep up.

"What the fuck you two stooges lookin' at? Cadence, like you don't bring Trinity flowers every Friday and, Wolf, don't get me started on how you treat a woman when they are in your life."

"Damn, Des, didn't think you had that kind of shit in you. that's why I'm shocked to shit. I know Trinity and Dee Dee like all women talk but Trin has never, in all the years we have been together, said your woman has shared your *'romantic side.'* That's what's freakin' me out, dude."

Watching these two idiots start to cackle again, I have had enough. Just as Trinity walk-waddles back in, I grab my credit card and hand it off to her.

"Darlin', can you book this for me for next weekend? The cabin on the computer screen is the one I want, if available, and add some champagne, snacks, and flowers. These two idiots know what I want if they can control themselves for a fuckin' minute. I would greatly appreciate it."

She looks up at me with shock in her eyes, but immediately after seeing my look, Trinity walks around the desk, tries to shove Wolf out of the chair until the big man just gets up, and starts reserving the cabin.

At least someone can take directions without giving me lip. I head out of the office toward the garage, knowing I won't be able to live this one down. But fuck it, it's gonna be worth it if I can give Dee Dee some time away from all of life's ups and downs. We're at our limit now.

Driving home to Dee Dee I'm smiling, 'cause I can't wait to share with her what I have set up. Well, with the help of Trinity and Wolf mainly. Our concerns for Daisy are taking over our lives 'cause we don't have a clue how to help her, and especially the situation is bothering Dee Dee who is feeling the emotional beatdown. Our lives have been hell for quite a while and we need a fuckin' break. So we are getting one. And Daisy is getting a mini vacation, as she will be staying with Trinity, Hope, and Cadence.

The one place she actually enjoys being anymore. And even if she doesn't want to go. she is going 'cause that young lady needs to chill out and I won't be taking no for an answer.

Pulling into our driveway, I am yet again amazed at how my life took that turn years ago when Dee Dee and I finally accepted we were meant to be. It has been wonderful but also work. A lot of goddamn work but I wouldn't change a damn thing. That woman owns my heart and soul. Before I even get out of my truck, Dee Dee is charging my way with a murderous look on her face. Holy shit, she looks beyond pissed. Nothing, not one word, comes out of my mouth. Fuck. Here we go again son of bitchin' drama at the home front.

"Des, she is going to be the death of me. When did my beautiful quiet daughter turn into the Tasmanian Devil with such a horrible bitchy attitude? I can't take much more, babe. She is literally killing me slowly. Every confrontation between the two of us pulls a bit more of my heart out of my chest. And that mouth of hers is either going to be the end of her or will see me in jail. She is such a mouthy brat lately."

Not wanting to share with her our plans for the next weekend in the driveway, but knowing in my soul she needs something, I give her what she needs.

Pulling her close, my hands move to grab her fine ass and hold her tightly to me as I lean down to her to place a kiss on those lips I love. She responds instantly with hands moving around my neck and her soft pliant body leaning into mine. I feel her body relax further as a sigh escapes from her beautiful lips.

"Sugar, hang on for a minute or two. Let's get inside first then we will deal with Daisy's latest drama, whatever the fuck it is. That girl is gonna have to figure her shit out and soon 'cause this bullshit can't keep going on. But know, woman, I have your back. We will get through this together."

Leaning back so she can look at my face, Dee Dee must like what she sees 'cause she face-plants into my chest as her hands go into my jeans pocket, holding me just a bit closer. Damn, she feels so fuckin' good. Knowing we can eventually handle any situation that comes our way, we head in to face our teenage daughter and today's drama.

CHAPTER TWO

DEE DEE

Thank God Des pulled into the driveway when he did. I was very close to strangling my youngest. Not sure where that attitude and lip came from, but I am at my wit's end. As we walk arm in arm into the house, I watch Daisy's lip curl up at the sight of us. As childish as it sounds I think to myself, *'whatever, kid.'*

"Des, wash up, dinner is ready. Jagger is working so it is just the three of us. Made your favorite, babe."

Smiling my way, he makes his way to the kitchen sink, grabbing Daisy by the neck, and giving her a kiss on the cheek. She grins his way but also pulls away almost immediately. I don't miss the look of concern that crosses his face before he blanks it.

I pull the meatloaf out of the oven to let it sit for a few, then grab the mashed potatoes to fill a serving dish, placing it on the table. Next I snag the broccoli and cauliflower, serving that up as well. By this time both Des and Daisy are sitting at the table. I throw the towel over my shoulder at the sink and take my seat. Like a rehearsed dance we say grace and then start filling our plates.

"My Sugar and Little Queen, how were your days? We were swamped at the garage. Not sure if it is the change in the season. With the ending of summer and fall around the corner, people are worried and want to service their cars. Ya know, before the cold weather."

His gaze sweeps first my way then to Daisy. She glances up at him, nods slightly, then concentrates on her plate. A plate that has two trees of broccoli, two pieces of cauliflower, and an end cut of meatloaf. No spuds. Go figure. God forbid she eat a carbohydrate. Stupid young girls always worried about their weight when they have no need to.

"Being I was off today, babe, I did the usual. Grocery shopping, cleaning, clothes, took the fur babies for their annual checkup. And made dinner. My usual day off."

Before Des can say a word, Daisy screeches across the table at me pissed as hell.

"Mom, why did you take the dogs and cats without me? You know I always go with and help.

That's always been our thing. See, this is a perfect example that you really don't want me around. Don't deny it either, you always actions speak louder than words."

She then leans back, crosses her arms, and shoots daggers my way.

"Hang on a minute, Daisy, your mom had the time. I doubt she intentionally left you out. Saying that, Little Queen, I want to talk to you both about something. I've been thinking and we all need a break. This household is like a war zone and I don't like it at all. So next weekend, Daisy, you are gonna spend time with Trinity, Hope, and Cadence. Sugar, we are going away for a couple of days."

My mouth drops open. What does that even mean? Go away, where, how, and more importantly why? Des is not a romantic type of guy; yeah, he can buy flowers or expensive gifts, but a spur of the moment couple's weekend? Nope, just not him, not him at all. This scares me so much but also piques my curiosity.

"Des, really, I can go for the weekend to the Powers' house? And spend time with little Hope? I would love that. We can hang out play with her Barbies, I can read to her, and maybe we can go to the park and maybe even get ice cream. Not to mention I can give Trinity a break because she is huge and probably needs some time for her before the twins come. What do you think, Mom, is that going to be okay? You cool with this?"

My head zips Daisy's way. She hasn't been this excited in a long time. Not to mention that smile on my beautiful girl's face. My heart warms just seeing her so happy. My man figured it out perfectly.

"Daisy, if you want to then yes, sweetie, I'm good with it. Des, what do you have planned for us? Hoping not another camping or cabin trip in the wild, no, you called it a nature trip. Just going to say the last one you surprised me with almost killed me with that poison ivy rash. Well, come on, give it to me."

Shaking his head and smiling his wicked sexy grin, I know he isn't going to share. Then he surprises me.

"Just to put you at ease, Dee Dee, I had help planning the weekend. That's all I'm gonna say. So now, Daisy, tell me about your day."

As we eat dinner, it is the first one in what feels like forever that is close to our old normal. That is a meal without a battle scene.

Later that evening after dinner, dishes, and some family TV, as Des is in the bathroom getting ready for bed, I walk down the hall to hear Daisy on the phone with who I assume is Trinity. Not intentionally eavesdropping, I'm shocked at my daughter's admission.

"Trinity, thanks for letting me come over next weekend. I truly appreciate. As do Mom and Des too. I've been a witch or the other word that starts with a b, so they probably need a break from my attitude and me. I can't wait to spend time with Hope and you. Can we get some ice cream? I know you've been craving it. Tell her I love her too and can't wait. See you guys soon."

Clearing my throat so she hears my approach, I walk through her bedroom door to her bedside.

"Thanks for helping with cleanup tonight, Daisy. Get some sleep 'kay?"

"You're welcome, Mom, and just so you know, I truly hope you have a great time on your weekend. Much deserved, I get it."

I grab my daughter by her neck and bend over so we are face-to-face.

"Baby, you need to know this. No matter what, you are a huge part of my heart and I love you. Even when we agree to disagree. You will have a wonderful weekend with Hope because it is all that girl will ever give to you. She adores you, Daisy. Night, honey."

Walking to our room, I first see bare feet then sleep pants and a Henley. My eyes reach Des's face, a face every time I see it takes my breath away.

"She okay, Sugar?"

"Actually, for once she seems to be. Maybe this too will pass. Where are we going, Des? You have to give me something so I know how do I pack, so again where are we going?"

"Dee Dee, pack for weather like we have, and you're not gonna need a lot of clothes, if you get my meaning. This is our weekend, Dee Dee, and I'm not taking you to wine country to taste different kinds of wine that's for sure. We're going somewhere to connect and enjoy each other. Bring what makes you comfortable. Not gonna tell you where we are going, 'cause it's a surprise. And, no, not even a blow job will get you the location."

Grinning like a lunatic, he grabs my hand and together we walk to our bed. We do this comfortably together, knowing what we have is real and special. And when my head hits the pillow, right before I fall asleep, I pray he didn't rent a frigging cabin in the woods with no electricity and water again. Couldn't handle that again, the last time almost did kill me.

CHAPTER THREE

DES

I can feel the trepidation and constant nerves rolling off Dee Dee as we continue to drive north. The morning started out good. I ran out early and got some donuts, so the family congregated in the kitchen, talking about the weekend. Daisy was so excited to spend it with Cadence, Trinity, and Hope. Jagger was thrilled Wolf asked him to help out at his ranch, so his time was going to be filled up.

Since both kids were going to be away, Dee Dee asked both Willow and Archie if they would stop by periodically and check on our fur babies. They did one better and they will be spending the weekend at our house. So everything fell right into place.

When we dropped Daisy off and both of my girls got emotional, which I thought was a good sign. They need a break with all that is going on with Daisy. Not normal teenage girl shit either. We just can't get a grip on whatever is going on. But the girl seemed happy today; maybe it was little Hope running right to her when we got there, a huge smile on her face. The plans she had would keep them both busy the entire weekend.

Once we got on the road, Dee Dee went quiet and that isn't like my woman. Not sure how to make her comfortable. My intentions were to give her a relaxing weekend not make her a nervous friggin' wreck.

"Sugar, quit fidgeting. I'm not takin' ya to a fuckin' sex club to tie you and spank your ass up all weekend. Well, unless that's what you want."

Turning just in time, I see her cheeks turn a pretty shade of pink. Well, fuck me senseless, didn't see that coming. Puttin' that on the list in the back of my mind definitely.

"Hon, I'm kidding, trust me, okay? I know the last couple of months have been rough with the garage and shop so busy and us shorthanded. Not to mention our kids with all of their teenage issues. I'm being selfish 'cause want you all to myself the entire weekend and can only hope you feel the same. That's what this is all about; quality time away to let our hair down and just chill. Reconnect. Okay?"

Nodding, she grabs my hand in hers, placing it on her upper thigh. And instantly I feel her body relax. Maybe I misread her anxiety. It could have been she was worried about Daisy and how she was going to react to today.

I follow the GPS for another ninety minutes until I see the first sign to the resort we are heading to. It's close to a small town where I thought we could take a leisurely walk around and check out the stores. Personally I hate to even walk into a shop, but Dee Dee is a master at it for Christ's sake. If there is a store she will end up in it.

Exiting right by the resort, I hear her pull in a deep breath and she lets go of my hand, putting both to her mouth.

"Oh no way. You didn't. Desmond Connelly booked a romantic weekend away? I can't believe it. This place looks awesome. Really. Wow."

She is babbling and I'm lovin' it. I did it, was able to take her out of her head. But I have to give credit where credit is due.

"Thank Trinity as I went to her for help. Told her what I was looking for, and she did the research and came up with this place. Well, actually, Wolf found the place have no clue how he did. Fingers crossed it lives up to everything that the online brochure stated. Don't be pissed at me though if it doesn't."

Hearing her laugh makes my day. Yeah, this was the right thing to do. I would do anything for my Sugar.

CHAPTER FOUR

DES

After parking and walking into the lobby, even my mouth drops. Damn, this place is the shit. Dee Dee is close, her arm around my waist, hand in my back pocket. Both of our heads are swinging back and forth, taking it all in. Total class. As I direct us to the reservation area, Dee Dee looks to her right and stops dead, clutching on to me so I also stop. Next to the desk is a beautiful table filled with all kinds of sweets and goodies displayed. My woman has a beautiful and smokin' body, but like all women she thinks she could lose some weight. I don't think that at all and would be pissed if she did. I give her a gentle push in that direction as I head to the desk.

"Good afternoon. Welcome to Serenity Springs. How may I assist you? And please, ma'am, help yourself to some refreshments. Please know, your room will have a similar display, on a smaller scale, for your pleasure. May I have the name the reservation is under?"

Watching Dee Dee walk to the table filled with sweets all excited almost skipping, I missed half of what the young chick said, but pull my credit card out and give her my name. As she processes everything, I turn my head and just the look on Dee Dee's face is worth whatever is being charged on my credit card. The stress of life in general and the last couple of months gone, she looks to be enjoying the little cake thing she is eating, if her soft moans are anything to go by. Instantly I feel my dick getting hard so I look away. Yeah, she continues to do that to me daily.

Trying to get into what Bobby, the front desk girl, is going over; I didn't realize all that was included in this weekend. Damn, all I wanted was a room with a king-size bed and Dee Dee. Reaching out, I grab the package Bobby presents to me with my credit card and the receipt. I don't look at it, afraid to, as she gives me directions on where our cabin suite is located. I thank her and head over to the goodie table. Dee Dee has two in her hands and a smile across her face.

"Sugar, go take a seat over in that section. I'm gonna pull the truck up and valet, so they can bring in our luggage. They will guide us to the cabin. Be right back."

She literally jumps my way, hands held out so I don't get chocolate on me, and gives me a huge smile, amber eyes sparkling.

"Des, so I don't forget, thank you for a wonderful weekend."

My heart skips a beat. I've accomplished my mission and even before I fucked my woman. Yeah, this weekend is gonna only get better.

As we follow the kid with our luggage, I can feel Dee Dee's excitement and it is getting me excited in more ways than one. Just watching her face full of happiness and joy fills my fuckin' heart. And knowing we have the entire weekend, just the two of us, gets other parts of me excited.

Coming to the end of the hall we exit the lodge, I notice the cabins seem to be farther apart. We walk for quite a bit on the path until the kid stops in front of Cabin 315 and inserts the keycard. Then he proceeds to open the door for us. Feeling kind of crazy in the moment, I lift my woman in my arms and carry her in, the entire time she is laughing hysterically. As soon as we pass through the door and enter the cabin, both of our eyes are huge as we take in the suite.

"Holy shit."

"Des, crap, this is stunning. And it's huge. What is this costing for the weekend?"

As Dee Dee and I go back and forth, the kid brings in the luggage off his cart and heads to the master bedroom, placing it in the luggage holders in the walk-in closet. Yeah, that room has a walk-in closet. He then goes back out and brings in a fruit basket and wine with glasses.

"Sir, Ma'am, this is on the house. Welcome to Serenity Springs. Let us know if there is anything you need. Your champagne is in the fridge. Call down to the lodge if you need assistance with it later. Enjoy your stay."

He goes to leave so I reach in, pull out some cash, and walk his way. He graciously accepts and thanks us again as he softly closes the door.

As I start to turn to my woman, out of the corner of my eye something flashes and then Dee Dee is flying toward me, hair cascading behind her. I put a foot back for balance and she actually lands and monkey climbs me until she has her legs around my waist, her hands holding behind my neck, pulling me down. Then her tongue is demanding entrance against my lips. My hands automatically grab her ass cheeks as I lift her higher and turn to balance her against the wall. My mouth opens as my tongue pushes hers back into her mouth, and I start to ravish her. I lean her into my body, so she can feel my hardness pushing into her soft center. She immediately mewls against my lips and literally starts to hump me. Moving against my hard as fuck cock. I lose all control and pull my mouth from hers.

"Hands up, Sugar, now."

She raises her arms and I instantly pull her top off. Pulling her back to me, I release her lacy bra and throw it to the floor. Next we both fight to undo our jeans, and I manage to get mine to my thighs as Dee Dee balances hands on my shoulders as she shimmies hers to her knees, and then one at a time down each leg. All this is done with her managing to stay in my arms.

As soon as she is ready, I grab her and she wraps those long-ass legs I love around me. I shift one hand to my weeping cock and in one movement push into her tight core feeling her walls tighten around me.

"Yes, oh God, Des, yes. Please fuck me. Fuck me hard."

The urgency in her voice makes me even harder, if that is even possible. Dee Dee doesn't generally swear so much so this is my clue she is way fuckin' turned on and lost all of her control. She pulls my hair 'cause I haven't given her what she wants. So I start to piston in and out of that tight warm pussy I call mine. I can feel the build low in my spine. Reaching between us, I feel how wet she is as I find her swollen clit. I roll it between my fingers and all her limbs tighten around me.

"God, Des, pleasssse don't stop. Yes, harder, baby, give it to me harder."

Fuck, how much harder does this woman want it? We might be leaving indentations or, worse, holes in the drywall now.

Grabbing her ass, I pull her closer and start thrusting and rolling my hips. Dee Dee has lost the little control she had as she is moaning, mewling, while trying to find her breath. Her hands have a death grip on my hair to the point of pain, and I pray she doesn't pull it out. Well, at this point I don't care. The heat is moving quickly down my spine into my balls and it is seconds before I lose it.

"Sugar, get there. Dee Dee, come now."

She pulls her head back, banging it on the wall again and again.

"Yes, yes, oh YESSSSSS."

Feeling her core tightening and milking me I give her one, two, three more thrusts and stay planted inside as I pour into her. I almost drop her my orgasm is so strong.

As we stay as close to each other as humans can be, I start to take in our situation and lightly laugh at first, but it quickly gets out of control.

"Damn, woman, not how I wanted this to go. Fuck, you jumped and monkey climbed me. I had this romantic plan and you just screwed it. Literally. Goddamn, Dee Dee, gotta give it to you, you continue to surprise me, gorgeous."

I feel her try to pull away but I keep her in my arms, still laughing. She buries her head in my neck and doesn't say a word.

"Sugar, just messing' with ya. We have the whole weekend. And, Dee Dee, you in my arms I have everything I need. You know that, right?"

She raises her head, a twinkle in her eye and huge smile on her face. I've been fooled.

"Gosh, Des, do you really think I'm that much of a sensitive Sally? That was the best wall banging we've done in a long time. You give good wall."

She roars with laughter as tears roll down her face. And watching I have no choice but to agree and laugh along with her. Great way to start our weekend.

CHAPTER FIVE

DEE DEE

After we clean up, Des and I sit down in the living room and eat the snacks and drink the wine. Neither of us are wine drinkers but it is pretty frigging good.

"Now what, Des? Do you have an itinerary or are we just winging it? By the way, again this is a beautiful cabin, babe."

"Sugar, since we got here earlier than I expected, do you want to go look around? Or we can go into town. For tonight, I didn't plan anything; wasn't sure how we were gonna feel. Tomorrow we have a couple's massage scheduled and a nice dinner. Besides that we are open. You know I'm up for just about anything. I'll willing to try whatever at least once or maybe twice if I enjoyed the first time."

My eyes fall to his crotch and then glance at Des with a twinkle in my eyes.

"Up for anything, huh?'

And I wink. Feeling playful, I want Des to know that he still gets my motor running. Even after the phenomenal wall banging.

He stalks to me, pulling me to him. His mouth is immediately on mine and I feel his warmth encompass me. His arms surround me, pulling my body into the hardness of his. I love the way he makes me feel. Safe. His tongue is lapping at my mouth as he nibbles on my lower lip. He gently kisses all over my face as his hands massage my back gently. I'm lulled into the web that is all that is Des. His taste and distinctive scent, which makes my blood start to heat up. He slowly disengages as he takes my hand and leads me down the hall to the master bedroom. I've never seen a bed so big or a room so lavish and luxurious. I'm in awe.

Des reverently removes each item of my clothing and then lowers me to the bed. He kneels between my legs gently pushing them apart. His eyes reveal everything, but as usual, Des knows exactly how to excite me.

"Sugar, gonna eat ya, then fuck ya, then repeat. That work for you?"

Eyes full of mischief, his mouth lowers until his tongue starts to worship at my altar. He eats like he is starving. My body bucks toward him as he uses his mouth, teeth, tongue, and fingers to let me know how much he is enjoying himself.

"Oh God, please, Des, don't stop. Yes, right there oh-oh-oh, yes."

Feeling my core tightening, I try to grasp on to his fingers as they move in and out in a rhythmic dance as old as time. I gasp for air as my hands grab on to the duvet, trying to hold on to the moment for as long as I can.

"Sugar, let go. I got ya. Always, Dee Dee, give it to me. Come, darlin."

My body tightens for a brief second or two then I fly. I feel his fingers pounding inside of me, finding that special place only he has ever touched. He sucks my sensitive nub into his mouth, increasing the overwhelming sensations running through my body. I am trembling with the intense orgasm coursing through my body. Des's touch becomes gentle as he prolongs my climax. When he feels me relax, he lifts and crawls up my body, kissing my tummy, breasts, and then nuzzles my neck.

"Sugar, you are so fuckin' beautiful when you come. Your entire body glistens, and the sounds. Goddamn, Dee Dee, I gotta fuck ya. I need to feel your warmth around me."

His hand is between us as he guides his steel hard cock into my pussy. I gasp as immediately I feel almost too full. His body is held taut, giving me some time. I need him as much as he needs me.

"Baby, please move. Don't treat me like a china doll. Please fuck me. I need you, Des. Now."

He starts grinding and pulling and pushing into me, as he talks dirty to me. Telling me everything he is going to do next and how good I feel. His words make my body hotter and hotter. My hands are running up and down his muscular back, ending at his phenomenal butt. I grab both muscular cheeks, letting him know to take what he needs.

"Jesus, Dee, I can't hold on. Please tell me you are there. Gonna blow, darlin'. Holy fuck, yes, you feel so tight and wet. What you do to me, Sugar. Come on, Dee Dee, get there. Milk my cock. Come on, that's it, oh yeah, that's my girl. Give it to me. All of it. Goddamn, yeah, oh yeah."

Des has lost control as he pounds into me, feeling my body release. His actions tell me he is close, so I pull his head down and whisper softly.

"Des, baby, that's it. I love that big hard cock of yours. I need you to come, Des. Please come."

His body instantly goes taut with his desire taking over. He gives me one, two, then on his third push he stays planted and I hear his growl as he fills me. His breath is coming fast and I can feel his heart pounding against my chest. He's giving me all of his weight, and even though it is crushing me, I love when he gives me everything. Wow, again what a start to a very promising weekend.

CHAPTER SIX

DES

God, between yesterday and today have been a total fuck-fest and my body is feeling it. No complaining, as Dee Dee has been insatiable and I love every minute of it. Yesterday after the wall bang and our tussle in bed, we cleaned up and went into town. Dee Dee had a blast, as she is a total crazy-ass shopper. I have to admit even I had a good time. We have gifts for everyone back home, which is crazy as we are only a couple of hours from them still in the same state. Dee Dee checked in with Trinity and Wolf on how the kids are doing. All is well for once. Willow and Archie also called to let us know our fur babies are good.

Feeling her, I turn from shaving and my mouth drops. Dee Dee saunters my way wearing a black lace demi bra and boy shorts. Oh my God the sight before me is beyond stunning. She approaches and before her body touches mine, her hand reaches for my semi-hard cock.

"Des, I feel the need to, ummmm, I need, well better if I just show you."

She kneels in front of me and immediately latches on to the head of my cock, licking the underside before taking me in deep. I feel the back of her throat as she hums. I instantly start to harden and between her mouth and hands, I know this isn't going to last but a quick minute. Dee Dee knows exactly how to take care of me. Her hands gently massage my balls then one hand grabs my ass and pulls me closer to her. I hear the moan come out of my mouth as my hips start to fuck her face. Pulling her hair back for a better view, I watch as she works my cock in and out of her hot as fuck mouth. I start to feel the burn down my spine just as Dee Dee's hand on my ass moves back down to my balls, squeezing them now with both hands. She is taking me down her throat and I know I'm not gonna last.

"Sugar, I'm gonna blow. Babe, shit oh God, not gonna last."

She moans against my cock on a downward glide and I feel her finger pressing in on my back hole. My body tenses as she pulls on her upward motion, and when she starts to move back down, I can feel the tip of her finger pressing into me from behind. My body immediately tenses for just a second or two and by the time she has me fully planted deep in her throat, my balls draw up and I shoot down her throat.

"Holy fuck! Goddamn, Dee Dee, I love that dirty little mouth of yours. Take it all—motherfucker—I can't stop. Yeah, baby, oh fuck yeah."

Dee Dee slows down her motion and gently cleans and licks me off before popping off my dick literally. I'm spent, feeling like I ran a marathon. Shit, my heart is literally pounding out of my chest.

"Sugar, I have no fuckin' words for what just happened. I need a minute or two to catch my breath."

She slowly stands up, grabbing my hand, pulling me out of the bathroom and onto the bed. We cuddle close and the last thing I remember before passing out is her soft words.

"Des, love you, baby. Thanks for this trip, you will never know how much it means to me."

I pull her closer and drift off to sleep.

Later that day, after our couple's massages, we took a walk around the property. I even surprised Dee Dee with a carriage ride through the park of the lodge.

I've got to say it was beautiful. We had a nice lunch starting with some wine and just enjoyed our time together. When we got back to the room, we took a short nap then a long-ass shower. I gave back to my woman for the earlier blow job, and if the nail marks on my shoulders are anything to go by, she appreciated my efforts.

Dinner was out of this world. The restaurant had to be close to or maybe even a five star. From the first moment we entered until we were done with dessert, it totally blew our minds. Never knew food could look or taste so good. Dee Dee had some kind of pasta dish while I had a ribeye steak. We tried each other's, and holy shit, I would drive back again just to go to the restaurant; it was that good. The appetizers, soup, and salad were also outstanding. And holy shit the desserts—as Dee Dee stated—they were orgasmic.

We sat in the lounge for a bit after dinner, listening to a live band, then hit the small casino on the property. Damn, we were on a roll, literally. Dee Dee won almost six hundred dollars on a slot machine and I didn't do too bad on the tables, coming out ahead close to a grand. Shit, just my winnings will help pay for this weekend. Not that I need it.

When we finally made it back to the room, we slowly took each other's clothes off and made love. We didn't rush and just let the mood take over.

Watching Dee Dee lose control and feeling her body react to mine was a feeling I will never take for granted. Ever. After I cleaned up my woman, turned out the light, and pulled her close, I realized how much we needed this weekend. Life can get so overwhelming and day-to-day chaotic. We needed to reconnect on this level so we know how lucky we are to have what we have.

"Dee Dee, thank you for trusting me enough with this weekend. I hope you know how much you mean to me. I love ya, darlin'."

"Des, this has been a perfect weekend. You surprised the crap out of me in a good way. I'm blessed in so many ways. My biggest blessing is having you in my and my kids' lives. I love ya too."

"Sugar, that's all we need. Our love is built on a solid relationship, which includes our family and the Horde. Let's get some sleep. Tomorrow is a new day."

With that, holding each other tight, we drift into a peaceful sleep knowing we can handle anything that comes our way. Together.

CHAPTER SEVEN

DEE DEE

Slowly waking up the heat that is surrounding me makes me second-guess opening my eyes. As my mind clears and thoughts come into focus, I hate today is our last day here. I've loved our weekend getaway and don't want it to end. Des shocked the hell out of me with his surprise. Feeling his morning wood pressed against my behind, I can tell he is still sleeping. Otherwise his cock would already be inside me. I smile to myself on that thought.

Gently I remove myself from the cocoon that is Des's body and make my way to the en suite. It is every woman's dream. I potty then brush my teeth and stare at the huge soaker tub. Yep, gonna get in that puppy before we leave. Quietly I leave the master bedroom area and head into the large family room, sitting in the corner of the large sectional, grabbing the room service book. After a couple of minutes I reach for the phone and place a huge order for us to start our day, which will definitely start with a huge carafe of hot coffee. They have a Keurig in the cabin that we have used and I'll probably make a quick cup while I wait for the food to get here. I need my morning nectar before I can start my day.

Getting back up I head into the kitchenette heading to the coffee station. Pulling out the cup drawer under the coffeemaker I search to see what kinds are left. Of course though, it is filled with every kind imaginable because room service fills it all the time. Feeling hands on my hips I scream bloody murder and elbow someone, well...yeah, duh Des, in the gut.

"Damn it, Des, you scared the crap out of me. You need to make some noise. I don't know, walk heavy or cough so I know you're coming toward me."

"Morning, Sugar, sorry bout that. You just look so fuckin' adorable in that robe and slippers, with your hair in that knotty thing. Give me a kiss, babe."

I turn and plant a hot one on my man. He grabs my shoulders, pulling me into his rock-hard body, taking my kiss to another level. I forget about my coffee and just about everything around us. As Des slowly finishes the kiss and pulls back, I follow his mouth not wanting to let him go. He chuckles.

Shaking my head I try to get my senses functioning again.

"Des, I ordered breakfast, was just going to make a quick cup of coffee to get my caffeine fix. Thought maybe I'd sit on the patio, it looks so peaceful out there."

He looks over his shoulder than back at me smiling.

"Go ahead, darlin', grab a throw and head outside. I'll make us both a cup and will meet ya out there."

Then he gently pushes me in the direction of the sectional, so I grab one of the throws off the back and head to the sliding glass doors. Pushing them open I immediately feel the cool morning air and move directly to the small loveseat, sitting down on it, and wrapping myself up in the fluffy blanket in my hands. I stare out into the beautiful start of the morning, realization hitting me that my man knew exactly what I needed. A time-out, I guess you can call it. Away from everything our family, the garage, and just the day-to-day BS that weighs ya down. I take in a deep breath of fresh clean air and hunker into the corner of the loveseat and just relax. Nothing comes immediately to my thought process so I just take in the view and enjoy the nothingness. Something new for me.

Hearing the sliding door pushing open I turn slightly to see Des approaching with the two coffees in his hands. He's put on some sleep pajama bottoms and a Henley 'cause it is brisk out here. Putting the cups down on the small table in front of us, he takes a seat, lifting the blanket, and pulling me right into his hard warm body. He tosses the throw over both of us and we just sit and enjoy the peace and serenity of the morning. Hearing the birds and start of a brand-new day makes me realize how I take so much for granted. Life is way too short and Des planning this little trip has shown me we have to take life by the pants and make it what we want. Yeah, the weekend together and all the sex is beyond wonderful, but this right here means more to me than anything. It shows me that Des not only knows me better than anyone else in my life, including me at times, but also can provide me with what I need.

"Sugar, what's goin' through that beautiful mind of yours? I can almost feel the wheels turnin'."

Looking up into that handsome face I fell for so many years ago as a young girl, I feel so blessed. We have had our ups and downs, as everyone does, but we have stuck it out. Now older and wiser we can enjoy each other fully.

"Des, I'm overwhelmed for some reason today. That you would go to this extreme to make sure I enjoyed myself blows me away. I've had such a great time, and not to be selfish, but it feels good not to have to worry about the day-to-day crap, not to mention all the stuff with our girl. I worry so much about Daisy, Des, but I don't know how to get in there. She has that wall built so thick and strong I can't break it. I'm afraid we are losing her. That would break my heart. Not sure what to do but when we get back, gotta figure out a way to reach her."

"Dee Dee, I totally agree. Gonna talk to Doc and Wolf when we get back. Especially Wolf since at his ranch he gives solace and a safe haven to those who've never had that before. Some of his folks are trained for shit like this, so maybe he can have a word with them and give us some direction."

Before he can say another word we hear not only the chimes from the doorbell but a soft knock at the door. We look to each other then, as if a choreographed dance, we both get up and head back into the cabin. I put our coffees on the table as Des goes to open the door. I hear his 'holy shit' as a waiter wheels in a cart filled high with I'm guessing is food. Dang, might have ordered a bit too much, but it all sounded so good. Looking to my man, he is shaking his head slightly as he reaches into the pocket of his sleep pants, and pulls out some cash to give to the young man who seems shocked when he looks down into his hand. Yeah, Des can come across rough and crap with his looks and tattoos but he's a softy deep down.

Once everything is set up on the table, we both sit and dig in. Not sure what today's plans are but looking forward to them, as this is our last day before reality hits us again right in the face.

CHAPTER EIGHT

DES

After our enormous breakfast we got dressed and decided to take a leisurely walk around the grounds. This resort is huge to say the least, so Dee Dee and I went exploring. We found not one but three small ponds that some folks were fishing by or just sitting around and relaxing. Down farther we heard it first but came upon a waterfall that was just beautiful. We decided to sit awhile and just enjoy the relaxing sounds of the water hitting the small man-made lake. It was surrounded by nature so Dee Dee got a kick out of the small animals, squirrels and chipmunks, who were carousing around the edge. We even saw what I think it was a beaver or something like that. My woman let out a loud shriek, so needless to say it took off like a bat out of hell. She laughs telling me she would try to be quiet so we can observe some more critters.

Sitting close and enjoying each other's company with out words made me realize how much this woman in my arms means to me. She is my calm in life's chaos. With the business, not to mention the Horde, life can be very tumultuous. Dee Dee brings a special kind of calm to my life. Something I've never had before her. Feeling her snuggling closer I feel the dampness and cool breeze.

"Come on, Sugar, you gettin' cold? Let's head back, maybe get a hot toddy or some hot cocoa, which ever you want."

She looks up at me all the love she has for me right there for me to see. I lean down and gently give her a kiss, hoping it relays all the feelings in my heart for her.

"Des, maybe we can hit up the front desk or go to the little shop and grab some goodies to go with our drinks? Since you extended our stay, might as well enjoy all the amenities, don't you think?"

Laughing I stand and pull my woman to me. Yeah, spoke to both Wolf and Cadence and we are gonna stay one more day. The guys have both Jagger and Daisy, so no worries there. According to Wolf both Willow and Archie are having a ball at our place with the fur babies. Got a feeling they are spoiling them rotten. Wolf did mention a couple of trips to the dog park, so again nothing to be too concerned about. We can enjoy today and then leisurely leave tomorrow and head back to our day-to-day. Gotta say though, I'm gonna keep this place in mind 'cause we will be comin' back.

Damn, can't eat another bite if someone paid for it. Glad we took that walk earlier and I didn't eat all that shit Dee Dee grabbed from the bakery. Dinner was fantastic. I've never had such a tender steak, not to mention those fuckin' shrimp were colossal. Feel like my gut is ready to explode.

I look over to see Dee Dee is also struggling. She ordered one of the specials, which was some kind of roast with all the fixings. And from what is left on her plate it was way too much. Not to mention the appetizer, soup, and salad we both munched down. And now they want to know if we want dessert. Holy shit.

"Darlin', go ahead, I'm gonna pass don't have an inch of room to put another goddamn thing in my mouth."

Watching Dee Dee's face fall, I know if I don't order something she won't either, and my woman loves her sweets. Shit.

Looking at the waitress I shake my head slightly then tell her to give us what is on the dessert list. She turns immediately and I see her grab a tray and head our way. Holy fuckin' shit. My eyes must be deceiving me. No way. Never saw so many choices before for such a small restaurant. This joint has it going on.

After we both listen to the many choices I decide on two for Christ's sake. Bread pudding and a blueberry cobbler with some vanilla ice cream on it. Not sure how I'm gonna squeeze this shit in my gut. Did tell our waitress to make them on the smaller side, like a half order, if at all possible. Dee Dee ordered some fancy-ass after dinner drink and a combination dessert plate that gives ya bite-size pieces of four items you get to pick out. We both are gonna be sick no doubt.

"Des, this has been a wonderful weekend. Does it make me a bad mom to say I wish we didn't have to go home tomorrow? I love our kids but I don't miss the drama. Well, I should say Daisy's drama, 'cause Jagger is just—ya know—so easygoing and comes and goes. Never heard him complain much and does whatever we tell him too. Daisy is another story."

"Sugar, we are gonna deal with everything that has been goin' on lately with our girl. First on my list is to speak to Wolf then Doc. We have the best resources at our fingertips. We'll get her back on track, promise. And, honey, glad you had a good time. I love being able to have ya all to myself, just sayin'."

I wiggle my eyebrows, which brings a giggle to her lips. As we sit back enjoying the rest of our evening, I can feel life is gonna be throwing some shit our way. Daisy has been all over the board lately, and it's gonna take everything we got to figure out what exactly is going on. Gonna enjoy these last couple of hours before we go back to 'real life.'

Rollin' off my woman, I'm strugglin' to catch my breath. Damn, that was out of this world. Feeling Dee Dee cuddling close, I put my arm around her, pulling her body so she is half on top of me. Listening to the sounds we are both makin' trying to recover from one hell of romp in the hay brings a smile to my face.

"What are you smiling about, Des?"

"Sugar, that was, fuck, got no words for it. You rocked my world, woman."

She giggles, shimmering closer, hand across my

abs. I feel when she relaxes and gives in to sleep 'cause I can feel her body let go against mine. My woman is done. I tighten my arms around her loving the feel of her softness on top of me. I lie here, with her wrapped in my arms, a thought again comes to mind that I'm one lucky son of a bitch. The conclusion is how very blessed I am. I've got my entire world in my arms and ain't never gonna let this woman go, no matter what bullshit is thrown our way. We've been through so much already and survived.

Eventually, after I manage to shut my brain off and I'm listening to Dee Dee's breathing, my body relaxes and my last thought before I fall into a calm and satisfied sleep is that I managed to hit this weekend out of the fuckin' park for Dee Dee. Gonna need to thank Wolf for finding this place.

Dee Dee

Suddenly jerking awake sometime later, in the middle of the night, I'm surrounded by Des and his heat. I shimmy even closer as a strange feeling of fear and the unknown fills my heart. Can't fight the apprehension that is making it hard to catch my breath. The brief nightmare that woke me was about Daisy. God I wish I could bring it all up but it's so fuzzy. It started a couple of years ago with Thanksgiving, when she got all upset about her music at Doc and Fern's and bit my head off. Since then she's been all over the board. We've tried to be there for her but nothing is working. All I know is in the nightmare one minute she was with us, and the next, she was gone. What does that even mean? Is this some sort of a sign or am I just so worried about my daughter that I'm making stuff up in my unconscious? I try to push it aside knowing Daisy is safe with Cadence and Trinity at this precise moment. I struggle to fall back asleep praying that everything will be all right. *Tomorrow is another day and all we can do is our very best*, I think this right before my mind shuts off and am able to get back to slumber.

Damn it, why do I let all this crap bring me down? I can't seem to reach the light no matter what I do. Winter break has had good and bad times. But just knowing tomorrow is time to go back to school is giving me huge frigging anxiety.

Mom and Des have tried really hard to just let me be. Like tonight at dinner, it must have showed on my face how much stress I was carrying because neither of them said one negative word. Not about my appearance, which I know I look like death warmed over. Not even about the lack of food on my plate. I did put some vegetables, salad, and two slices of roast. No bread or potatoes though. Des watched me closely throughout the meal, but said not a word. And shock of all shocks, Mom didn't ride my ass either. And thank God Jagger was at work.

Now I'm in my bedroom trying to figure out what to wear tomorrow. Since my weight loss progress, most of my clothes are baggy. And yes, that's a good thing, but also not because I can't let Mom see the clothes hanging off of me or she will get up in my business yet again. I search my closet and find a pair of old jeans, way in the back. I think I wore these in seventh grade, but fingers crossed I might be able to squeeze into them. That solves the bottom half now the top remains. I can probably get away with a T-shirt and hoodie and they should be a bit baggy as no one wears skintight hoodies. I have a plan I think to myself and smile.

After getting my clothes in order, I work on my book bag and make sure everything I need for tomorrow is in there. Also have my small bottle of mouthwash, Tums, hand wipes, and Band-Aids. Gotta be prepared, no matter what. The first two in case I need to purge for whatever reason. The next one, the wipes, for not only cleaning after said purging but also if one of my cuts breaks open and starts to bleed. That is also why I have Band-Aids. You can never be too careful.

Thinking on that, gonna take a shower tonight because I'm definitely not a morning person. Especially with not being able to sleep much lately. I can be extremely tired and then I get in bed and it's like suddenly I'm wired and can't for the life of me fall to sleep. No matter what, I've counted sheep, drank warm milk, and even taken that melatonin stuff. Crazy, don't even know why I'm not able to fall asleep 'cause I'm exhausted all the time. Not to mention the constant pain I feel in all parts of my body, especially my tummy and where all my cuts are. Also thinking some of them are either infected or on the road to being infected. My life sucks big time.

Daisy's Darkness is up next in the series. Get your copy here [Daisy's Darkness (Book 6)](#)

ABOUT THE AUTHOR

USA Today Bestselling author D. M. Earl spins stories about real life situations with characters that are authentic, genuine and sincere. Each story allows the characters to come to life with each turn of the page while they try to find their HEA through much drama and angst.

When not writing, DM loves to read some of her favorite authors books. Also she loves to spend quality time with her hubby & family along with her 7 fur babies. When weather permits she likes to ride her Harley.

Contact D.M at DM@DMEARL.COM
Website: http://www.dmearl.com/

- facebook.com/DMEarlAuthorIndie
- twitter.com/dmearl
- instagram.com/dmearl14
- amazon.com/D-M-Earl/e/B00M2HB12U
- bookbub.com/authors/d-m-earl
- goodreads.com/dmearl
- pinterest.com/dauthor

ALSO BY D.M. EARL

DEVIL'S HANDMAIDENS MC: TIMBER-GHOST, MONTANA CHAPTER

Tink (Book #1)

GRIMM WOLVES MC SERIES

Behemoth (Book 1)

Bottom of the Chains-Prospect (Book 2)

Santa...Nope The Grimm Wolves (Book 3)

Keeping Secrets-Prospect (Book 4)

A Tormented Man's Soul: Part One (Book 5)

Triad Resumption: Part Two (Book 6)

WHEELS & HOGS SERIES

Connelly's Horde (Book 1)

Cadence Reflection (Book 2)

Gabriel's Treasure (Book 3)

Holidays with the Horde (Book 4)

My Sugar (Book 5)

Daisy's Darkness (Book 6)

THE JOURNALS TRILOGY

Anguish (Book 1)

Vengeance (Book 2)

Awakening (Book 3)

STAND ALONE TITLES

Survivor: A Salvation Society Novel

Printed in Great Britain
by Amazon